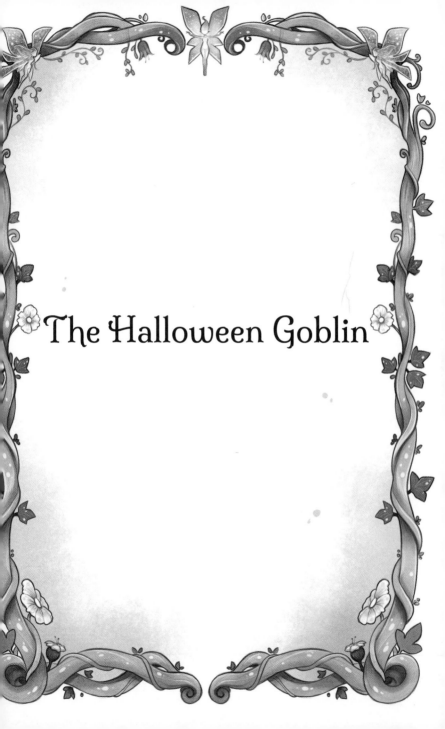

The Halloween Goblin

Pixie Tricks

Read All the Magical Adventures!

Pixie ★ Tricks

The Halloween Goblin

Written by
Tracey West

Illustrated by
Xavier Bonet

SCHOLASTIC INC.

This book is in memory of my friend Dan,
who loved all things spooky. —TW
For my children, Daniel and Marti.
You're pure magic. —XB

Text copyright © 2000, 2021 by Tracey West
Illustrations copyright © 2021 by Xavier Bonet

Library of Congress Cataloging-in-Publication Data
Names: West, Tracey, 1965- author. | Bonet, Xavier, illustrator. | West, Tracey, 1965- Pixie tricks ; 4.
Title: The Halloween goblin / written by Tracey West ; illustrated by Xavier Bonet.
Description: [New edition, with new illustrations] | New York : Branches/Scholastic Inc., 2021. |
Series: Pixie tricks ; 4 | Originally published: New York : Scholastic, © 2000. |
Summary: Two pixies are double trouble for Violet, Leon, and their fairy friend Sprite; they have to find a way to trick Bogey Bill, a goblin who loves Halloween and scaring people, and Buttercup who has cast a spell on the whole school that has all the children hiccupping uncontrollably—and with the help of a good fairy named Robert B. Gnome they come up with a way to deal with both at once.

Identifiers: LCCN 2020040126 (print) | ISBN 9781338627879 (paperback) |
ISBN 9781338627886 (library binding) |
Subjects: LCSH: Fairies—Juvenile fiction. | Goblins—Juvenile fiction. | Halloween—Juvenile fiction. |
CYAC: Fairies—Fiction. | Goblins—Fiction. | Halloween—Fiction.
Classification: LCC PZ7.W51937 Hal 2021 (print) | LCC PZ7.W51937 (ebook) | DDC 813.54 [Fic]—dc23
LC record available at https://lccn.loc.gov/2020040126

10 9 8 7 6 5 4 3 2 1   21 22 23 24 25

Printed in China   62
This edition first printing, September 2021
Book design by Sarah Dvojack

Table of Contents

Whenever pixies do escape
Through the old oak tree,
Here is what you have to do
Or trouble there will be.
First find a Pixie Tricker,
The youngest in the land.
Send him to the human world,
The Book of Tricks in hand.
Once he's there, he'll find a girl
Who's only eight years old.
But she's a smart and clever girl
Who's also very bold.
He must ask her for her help,
And if she does agree,
They'll trick the pixies one by one
Till no more do they see.
Only they can do the job.
It's much more than a game.
For if they fail to trick them all,
The world won't be the same!

1

Eleven More to Go

"Thank you for letting me come to school with you today," Sprite said. The little green fairy sat on Violet's shoulder, tucked behind her red ponytail. His rainbow wings brushed against her freckled cheek.

"Just remember to stay hidden when we get there," Violet said. "Nobody else in school knows that fairies are real."

Violet's cousin ran up to them. Leon had dark eyes and curly brown hair.

"Can we go pixie tricking after school?" he asked.

"We need to!" Sprite said. "We have only tricked three fairies so far. We still have eleven more to go!"

Violet looked down at her shirt. It was blue with a big purple flower on it. "Maybe I shouldn't have worn my brand-new shirt today. Pixie tricking can be messy!"

"It's a pretty shirt," Sprite said.

Violet smiled. "Thank you, Sprite," she said.

Leon pointed to his shirt. It had a wizard on it. "Do you like my shirt, Sprite?"

Sprite shuddered. "No! That face reminds me of Finn the Wizard. Finn led the pixies when they escaped from the fairy world. And now he's out to get us!"

"Why is he after us?" Leon asked.

"Finn wants us to stop tricking pixies," Sprite replied. "He likes making trouble in the human world. I think he's planning to do something big. And bad."

Leon held up his fists. "Well, I'm not afraid of some old wizard!"

"You should be," Sprite warned. "Finn is very powerful!"

Violet looked down at Sprite on her shoulder. "You'd better get in my backpack," she said. "We're almost at school."

A crowd of children waited on the corner. The crossing guard held them all back.

"Wait here!" the woman said nervously. "Crossing the street is very dangerous. Cars racing. Trucks zooming. Watch out! Watch out!"

But there wasn't a car or truck in sight.

"That's strange," Violet said.

Sprite peeked out of the backpack.

"What's strange?" he asked.

"The crossing guard is acting weird," Violet said. "She—"

"Violet!" Leon cried. "Your shirt!"

Violet looked down at her shirt. And she screamed!

5

2
Monster Alert!

Instead of a purple flower, there was a picture of a purple monster's face on Violet's shirt! The face had long fangs. It had bulging eyes. Slime dripped from its hairy ears.

"Blaaaaah!" the monster face growled! It stuck out its tongue.

"Yikes!" yelled Violet.

"Is your shirt supposed to do that?" Leon asked.

"Definitely not!" Violet replied. She moved to the edge of the sidewalk. She didn't want anyone to hear them talking about pixies. More kids had lined up behind the crossing guard. She still wasn't letting anyone cross.

"Leon," Violet said, "the monster on my shirt is *moving*! Something's going on here!"

Sprite flew out of the backpack. "I think I know who did this. The crossing guard is scared. The flower on your shirt became something scary. It has to be . . ."

"Happy Halloween!" a voice growled.

7

There was a flash of gray. A small creature darted into the bushes next to them. It ran out of sight.

"Bogey Bill!" Sprite cried. "I knew it!"

"Bogey who? Was that another fairy?"
Leon asked. "And why did he say, 'Happy
Halloween'? Halloween isn't for weeks and
weeks."

"Bogey Bill is a goblin—a fairy who likes to scare people," Sprite said. "He wishes every day were Halloween. He has two main powers. He can make people feel afraid for no reason. And he can turn normal things into scary things."

Violet looked down at the monster face. "Well, that explains my shirt. Can we fix it?"

Sprite fluttered his wings. "I'm not sure," he said.

"What if I say Bogey Bill's name backward three times?" Violet asked. "That has stopped pixie magic before."

"You could try," Sprite said.

Violet took a deep breath.

"Llib Yegob!

"Llib Yegob!

"Llib—*hic*!"

"Hic?" Sprite asked. "Violet, you said it wrong."

Violet moaned. "I—*hic*—know!" she said.

"You have the hiccups, Violet," Leon said. "Let me try."

Leon pointed at Violet's shirt. "Llib Yegob! Llib Yegob! Llib Yegob!"

The monster face sparkled. Then it turned back into a purple flower!

"I did it!" Leon cried. "I saved the day."

"Thanks—*hic*!" Violet said. "Now maybe you can try and fix the crossing guard so we can all cross the street."

"I'm on it!" Leon said. He ran over to the crossing guard and shouted at her, "LLIB YEGOB! LLIB YEGOB! LLIB YEGOB!"

Some kids started laughing. The crossing guard looked confused.

"What did you—oh my, so many kids!" she said. She looked both ways and stepped out into the empty street. "Cross, everyone!"

Sprite slipped back into the backpack. Violet caught up to Leon and they crossed the street.

"Nice work—*hic*! Now stay on the lookout for Bogey Bill," Violet whispered to Leon. "If he shows up at school, there will be trouble!"

3
Hic—Trouble!

When Violet and Leon got to class, they took their seats. Then Violet slipped Sprite inside her desk. She made sure no one saw him.

"*Hic.* Are you all right?" Violet whispered.

Sprite stretched out on top of Violet's box of pencils.

"There's not much to do here," Sprite whispered back. "But that's okay. I've got to think about how to trick Bogey Bill."

Sprite took a tiny book from his bag. *The Book of Tricks.* The book told how to trick the escaped pixies.

"Good luck. *Hic!*" Violet said.

Suddenly, Violet got goose bumps on her arms. She shivered. *Is Bogey Bill here?* she wondered.

Before she could get up and look for him, the bell rang. Their teacher, Ms. Rose, took attendance. Violet liked Ms. Rose. She always wore bright colors. And she smiled a lot.

But today Ms. Rose wasn't smiling. She looked nervous. She tapped her fingers on the desk.

"Leon, can you please go to the supply closet for me?" Ms. Rose asked.

Leon looked scared. He stared at the closet door. He didn't move.

"Ms. Rose, do I have to?" Leon asked.

"Is something wrong?" the teacher asked.

"Uh, no," Leon said. He looked pale. "I—I just don't want to."

Ms. Rose smiled nervously. "Who would like to open the closet door for me?"

No one in the class answered. They all looked scared. Even Violet was scared, but she didn't know why.

Ms. Rose took a deep breath. "I guess I'll do it myself, then," she said.

Ms. Rose walked to the closet. She grabbed the doorknob.

Violet turned her head. She couldn't look. None of the kids in class could look, either.

Ms. Rose slowly turned the knob. She opened the door.

Then she smiled. "See, class?" she said. "Nothing to be scared of."

Violet turned around. There was nothing in the closet but paper and paint.

Ms. Rose picked up some orange and black paper.

"Today we will make Halloween decorations," the teacher told the class. She started to pass out the paper.

Halloween decorations? Violet thought. She gasped. *Bogey Bill must be near! He made us all feel afraid of the closet. And somehow he has made Ms. Rose think it's Halloween!*

Violet raised her hand. "Um, Ms. Rose, it's not Hallo-*hic*! *Hic!*"

"Violet Briggs has the hiccups!" Evan Peters chanted.

Ms. Rose frowned. "It's not nice to tease, Evan. Please apologize to Violet."

Evan rolled his eyes. "Sorry, Violet. *Hic!*"

Some of the kids giggled.

Ms. Rose looked angry. "Evan, I warned you!"

But Evan looked shocked. "*Hic!* I really do have the hiccups. *Hic!*"

Then the sound of hiccups filled the room.

Violet couldn't believe it. *Now my whole class has the hiccups? This sounds like fairy magic to me!*

4
Lunchtime Surprise

Violet leaned down to talk to Sprite. The class was too busy hiccuping to notice.

"Sprite!" Violet whispered. "What—*hic*—is going on? Is it Bogey Bill?"

"Bogey Bill is making everyone feel afraid," Sprite replied. "But he doesn't cause hiccups."

"*Hic!* So who does?" Violet asked.

"I'm not sure," Sprite said. "But it looks like we might have to trick two pixies this time! Let me check *The Book of Tricks.*"

"All right—*hic*—class!" Ms. Rose said. "Let's get to work on those decorations!"

Violet's class hiccupped all morning long. Finally, it was time for lunch.

Violet slipped Sprite into her lunch bag. She wanted to go somewhere and talk to him. She wanted to find out what he had learned from *The Book of Tricks*.

But her friend Brittany Brightman ran up to her as they walked to the lunchroom. Brittany had friendly brown eyes behind wire-rimmed glasses. And she wore her black hair in a long braid.

"Violet! You're coming over to help me play with Ruby today, right?" Brittany asked.

"Oh, I forgot!" Violet said. Ruby was Brittany's three-year-old sister. "Um, I'm supposed to do something with Leon . . ."

"But you *have* to—*hic*—help," Brittany said. "You always make Ruby laugh. Besides, my dad said he talked to your mom about it."

Violet nodded. "Okay, I'll be there!" *I hope Leon and Sprite understand!* she thought.

The girls sat down at their table. Violet looked around. The sound of hiccups filled the room.

Kids were doing all kinds of things to get rid of their hiccups. They were holding their noses and

drinking milk. One boy was standing on his head.

Everyone was trying to eat the Friday lunch special—spaghetti. But they were hiccupping too much to get the food in their mouths.

Suddenly, the hiccups stopped.

"Eek!" a girl yelled. "My spaghetti is alive!"

"So is mine!" cried a boy.

Violet looked across the whole lunchroom. Spaghetti was crawling around on everyone's plates, like worms!

The kids and lunch aides started to scream. Even Leon was screaming. Violet ran to him.

"Bogey Bill must be doing this," she said. "We have to stop this spell!"

"I have an idea," Leon said. He stood on a table. "Everybody repeat after me! Llib Yegob!"

"Why should we do that?" someone shouted.

"Just try it!" Leon cried. "Llib Yegob!"

As everyone chanted, Violet ran into the hall with her lunch bag.

"Sprite!" she said. "What have you found out about Bogey Bill? *Hic!*"

Sprite flew out of the bag. He opened *The Book of Tricks*.

Violet saw the page about Bogey Bill. There was a blank space where his picture should be. Violet knew that the picture would reappear when Bogey Bill was tricked.

There was also a short rhyme. Sprite read it out loud.

This goblin wants to scare you.
He thinks spooky things are neat.
If you want to trick him,
Make him say something sweet.

"How can we trick him when we can't even see him?" Violet asked.

She peeked inside the lunchroom. Saying Bogey Bill's name backward had worked again. The spaghetti had stopped moving. Nobody was afraid anymore. But they were confused.

"What just happened?" Brittany asked. "Leon, what did those words mean?"

"Um . . ." Leon said.

"Uh-oh," Violet said. "How are we going to—*hic*—explain this?"

5

Snakes Alive!

"I think I can make everyone forget about what just happened," Sprite said.

"Do it!" Violet urged him.

Sprite blew pixie dust into the room.

"On your mark, get set, get ready! Forget about that weird spaghetti!" he chanted.

The glittering dust swirled around the lunchroom. The kids and lunch aides blinked. Then the kids began eating their spaghetti like nothing had happened.

"Good job, Sprite! *Hic!*" Violet said. He flew back into her lunch bag.

She walked up to Leon.

"I saved the day again!" Leon said. "And the best thing is, nobody has the hiccups anymore. The spaghetti worms scared the hiccups right out of them."

"I've still got them—*hic*!" Violet said. "The worms didn't scare me because I knew Bogey Bill was doing it."

"Well, they still scared me," Leon admitted. "We've got to find Bogey Bill and trick him after school! He could scare everybody in town!"

"Yes, we must hurry," Sprite agreed.

"I can't," Violet said. "*Hic!* I have to help Brittany watch her baby sister."

Leon frowned. "Do you have to?"

Violet nodded. "I promised!"

"While you are busy, Leon and I can find out who is causing the hiccups," Sprite said.

"Good idea," Violet agreed.

Nothing scary happened for the rest of the school day. Nobody else but Violet hiccupped. Ms. Rose forgot about making Halloween decorations.

After school, Violet and Brittany walked to Brittany's house.

Brittany's dad greeted them when they got inside.

"Thanks for playing with Ruby today, girls," Mr. Brightman said. "I've got an important call. If you can keep her busy for me, that would be a big help."

Ruby ran up to Violet and hugged her knees. She had black, curly hair and big, brown eyes. "Hi, Violet!" she said. She held out a pink stuffed bunny rabbit. "It's Fluffy Bunny time!"

Violet looked at Brittany. "What's Fluffy Bunny time? *Hic!*"

Ruby laughed at the sound of Violet's hiccups.

"It's Ruby's favorite show," Brittany said. "*The Fluffy Bunny Show.* I think it's silly, but Ruby loves it."

She turned on the TV. A person in a big pink bunny outfit was singing a song.

Ruby sang along. "Carrots are orange, carrots are sweet! Carrots are good to eat!"

Brittany rolled her eyes. "See what I mean?" she asked. "But Ruby and all the kids in her playgroup love it. Tomorrow is the big *Fluffy Bunny Show* live special. They're all going to watch it together."

Fluffy Bunny sang the song again. Brittany held her ears and turned away from the TV. "I can't stand it!"

But Violet smiled. She'd rather watch a fluffy pink bunny than look for a scary fairy. This was a lot safer.

"*Hic!* I like Fluffy Bunny," Violet said. "He's cute. Right, Ruby?"

Violet gasped. The toy bunny in Ruby's hands had changed. Now it was a stuffed snake!

Ruby saw Violet's shocked face. She looked at her stuffed toy.

Then she began to cry. "Waaaaaaaaah!"

Brittany turned to her little sister. "What's wrong?"

Violet quickly grabbed the snake from Ruby. Then she started to hiccup. "*Hic! Hic! Hic!*"

Ruby laughed, and Brittany shook her head. "Let me get you some water, Violet."

Brittany left the room. Violet looked at the stuffed snake. "Llib Yegob! Llib Yegob! Llib Yegob! *Hic!*"

The snake turned back into a bunny. Violet gave it to Ruby.

"Bad bunny!" Ruby said.

But Violet knew it wasn't the bunny's fault. Bogey Bill had struck again!

The goblin didn't show up anymore that day. Violet stayed for dinner at the Brightmans' house.

When she got home, Sprite was sleeping soundly in her sock drawer. Leon was busy playing video games.

Tomorrow, we'll figure out a plan to stop that scary fairy! she thought.

6
Queen Mab

The next morning, Violet woke up to Sprite's wings tickling her face. She giggled.

"Good morning, Sprite! *Hic!*" she said.

"Good morning!" Sprite replied. "I have news. Last night, Leon and I found out who is causing the hiccups. She is a flower fairy named Buttercup."

He held up *The Book of Tricks* and read out loud.

She will give you the hiccups,
Anytime or anywhere.
To trick this silly sprite,
You must give her a big scare!

"That makes sense," Violet said. "A good scare is one way to get rid of hiccups. Now we know how to trick Buttercup."

Sprite flew away from her face. "Let's go look for her now!"

"Breakfast first," Violet told him. "*Hic!*"

After they ate, Violet and Sprite tried to wake up Leon. Violet shook him. Sprite tickled Leon's face with his wings. But Leon only grumbled and pulled the covers over his head.

"He can catch up to us later. *Hic!*" Violet said, as she walked outside. "Let's look for Bogey Bill first."

Sprite flew onto Violet's shoulder. "We should find Buttercup, too. You need to get rid of those hiccups."

"I know," Violet said. "But Bogey Bill is worse. *Hic!*"

Just then, Violet noticed something. A soft purple light shone through Sprite's magic bag.

"The fairy queen!" Violet said. "She can help us. *Hic!*" Queen Mab had helped them the last time they had a problem.

Sprite opened the bag and took out a small stone. The stone glowed brightly.

The glow quickly faded. Then a picture began to appear.

It was Queen Mab. Violet had forgotten how beautiful she was. She had long, pink hair, purple eyes, and brown skin.

Sprite and Violet bowed.

"Greetings, Queen Mab," Violet said. "It's good to see you. We could use your help."

"That is why I am here. What can I do for you?" asked the fairy queen.

Sprite lowered his eyes. "We're a little, um, confused," he said. "Two pixies are causing trouble at the same time."

"And we don't know how to find either of them," Violet added. "*Hic!*"

"We've got to trick Buttercup and Bogey
Bill!" said Sprite. "But Bogey Bill is so scary."

Queen Mab thought. "I know someone
who is not afraid of Bogey Bill," she said.
"Robert B. Gnome can help you."

"Who is he?" Sprite asked. "And how do we find him?"

The queen's picture faded. In its place was a picture of a tiny little man. The chubby gnome had a smiling face and blue eyes. He had pink cheeks and a white beard. He wore a pointy red cap on his head. And he was in a flower garden.

"I've seen that gnome before. *Hic!*" Violet said.

They could still hear the queen's voice. "Robert is a good fairy. He has lived in your world for years, Violet," she said. "Go to him. He can help you."

Then the stone went dark.

"What are we waiting for?" Sprite asked. "Let's go see Robert B. Gnome!"

7
Robert B. Gnome

"There's a house around the corner with a nice garden," Violet explained. "I've seen Robert B. Gnome there."

Sprite followed Violet down the street to a tiny white house. Many colorful flowers grew in the garden.

A small statue stood in front of a rosebush. The statue looked just like the gnome Queen Mab had shown them. He had a red cap. A big smile. A white beard.

"There's only one problem," Sprite said. "That gnome is not real! He's a statue."

The gnome stood still. His hands were on his hips.

Violet knelt down next to the statue. "*Hic!*
It has to be him. It looks just like him."

Sprite flew in front of the statue's face. "Are
you Robert B. Gnome?"

"*Achoo!*"

Violet jumped back. "Did that statue just
sneeze?" she asked.

"Achoo!"

The little man chuckled. He raised both arms and scratched his nose.

"Those wings of yours sure are ticklish," he said in a jolly voice.

"Robert B. Gnome!" Violet said. "I knew it was you!"

The gnome grinned. "That's me! I am usually careful to stay still in front of humans. But then I saw you talking to this little fellow here."

"I'm Sprite," Sprite said. "I'm a Royal Pixie Tricker."

"How can I help you?" the gnome asked.

Violet and Sprite told the gnome about Bogey Bill and Buttercup.

Robert B. Gnome stroked his beard. "That Bogey Bill," he said, shaking his head. "He and I grew up together. I knew that goblin when he couldn't even scare a grasshopper."

"We know what we're supposed to do to trick him and Buttercup," Sprite said. "But we're not exactly sure *how* we trick them."

"*Hic!* And we don't know where to find them, either," Violet said. "We saw Bogey Bill for a—*hic*—second. And we have never seen Buttercup."

The gnome stroked his beard some more.

"You've got two pixies to trick," he said. "That's double trouble."

"You can say that again," Sprite said.

"But it is also double good," Robert B. Gnome said. "You can use their powers against each other."

"*Hic!*" Violet said. "How do we do that?"

"Oh, you'll know," said the gnome. "When the time comes, you'll know."

Robert B. Gnome took off his red cap. He rummaged through it. Then he pulled out a small stuffed toy. A spider. "Take this," he said. He handed the toy to Violet. "You might be able to use it."

"*Hic!* Thanks," Violet said. "What should we do next?"

"If I were Bogey Bill, I'd probably be in the scariest place in town," the gnome replied. "You should go there."

Sprite's wings fluttered faster than ever. "Can't you tell us more?"

But Robert B. Gnome smiled. "You'll be just fine," he said. "Now I've got to get back to guarding this garden."

And suddenly the gnome was as still as a statue again.

"This is confusing," Sprite said. "What are we supposed to do with a stuffed spider? And how are we supposed to bring the two fairies together?"

Violet frowned, thinking. Then her face lit up. "I know where to start! Robert B. Gnome said to look in the scariest place in town. *Hic!* There's an old house near the park. It's the spookiest place around."

Sprite shivered. "Are you sure it's a good idea to go to a spooky—aaaaah!"

Something jumped out in front of them!

8

The Spooky House

"You snuck off without me!"

Violet relaxed. It wasn't Bogey Bill.

It was Leon.

"You were asleep," Violet said. "We tried to wake you up."

Leon yawned. "I was up all night playing a video game. But I'm here now."

"Good, because we have a plan," Violet said. She told him about Robert B. Gnome.

She showed Leon the stuffed spider. "I'm still not sure what to do with this," she said.

"I'll hold on to it," Leon said. "It's cool." He jammed it into a pocket of his shorts.

"Let's go to that creepy old house by the park," Violet said. "The one that's been empty for years. I think we'll find Bogey Bill there."

Then Violet stopped. "Hey! My hiccups are gone!"

"That's right!" Sprite said.

"It's because I scared you," Leon explained. "You should thank me."

"Thank you!" she said. "*Now* I know how to trick Buttercup. Let's get moving!"

Sprite reached for his bag of magical pixie dust. The dust would take them anywhere they wanted to go. In a flash.

Sprite threw the pixie dust on them.

Violet held her nose so she wouldn't sneeze. Her body tingled as the garden disappeared.

They appeared in front of a tall house.
It looked old and gray, and had boarded-up
windows.

Violet and Leon walked up the worn,
creaky steps. Sprite flew alongside.

Leon stopped. "Um, are you sure we should
go in here?"

"We can't be afraid," Violet said. "We have
pixies to trick."

They opened the door and walked into a dark room. The room was filled with dusty furniture. An old piano sat against one wall. A chandelier hung from the ceiling.

"This is the perfect place for Bogey Bill," Violet whispered.

Then a cold wind blew through the room. The tattered curtains fluttered. The piano played a tune all by itself. The chandelier swung back and forth.

Bam! There was a loud crash behind them!

9
A Trap for Buttercup

Violet spun around. A picture had fallen off the wall. The glass in the frame had broken into pieces.

"Must have been the wind," Violet said.

"Or Bogey Bill," Leon added.

"Maybe it was," Violet agreed. Then she whispered to Leon and Sprite, "Robert B. Gnome said that we could use the powers of Buttercup and Bogey Bill against each other. We just need to get Buttercup to come here."

"How are we going to do that?" Leon asked.

Violet looked at her cousin. "I have a plan."
Then she started talking in her loudest voice.
"Hey, my hiccups are gone! I'm so happy I
don't have hiccups!"

Nothing happened.

Violet raised her voice.

"No more hiccups for me!" she said. "I'm
so lucky!"

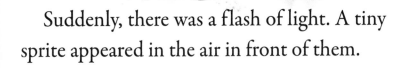

Suddenly, there was a flash of light. A tiny
sprite appeared in the air in front of them.

Violet was amazed each time she saw a fairy. This one had skin the color of an acorn. Her hair and dress were made of yellow flower petals. She wore green boots.

"Buttercup!" Violet cried.

"Stop saying bad things about hiccups!" said the fairy, fluttering her shiny wings. "Hiccups are wonderful things. They sound beautiful. I *love* hiccups!"

"I hate them," Violet said. "I'm glad to be rid of them."

Buttercup frowned. She stomped her tiny foot in the air.

"What a terrible thing to say," she said. "I'll give you the hiccups again. I'll show you how nice they are!"

A silver wand popped into Buttercup's hand. She waved the wand in front of Violet. "I will give you hiccups that last forever!" Buttercup cried.

"Violet, we should get out of here!" Leon yelled.

Violet didn't move. She hoped that her plan was going to work.

She got her wish.
"Happy Halloween!" a voice growled.
Bogey Bill crashed through the ceiling.

Violet gasped. Bogey Bill was a very scary-looking fairy! He had yellow eyes and sharp teeth. His skin was gray. He had very big feet and very long, pointy ears.

Bogey Bill stuck out his tongue and made a terrible face. His yellow eyes glared at them. "Eeeeeeeeeek!" screamed Buttercup.

10
Get That Goblin!

A whooshing sound filled the air. A tunnel of wind appeared out of nowhere. The wind sucked Buttercup inside.

"I love hiccups!" Buttercup yelled. "Is that so w-w-r-o-n-n-g-g . . . ?"

Then the room was quiet. Buttercup and the tunnel vanished.

"Yes!" Leon cheered.

"We did it!" Violet said. "Bogey Bill scared Buttercup! We tricked her and sent her back to the Otherworld!"

But it wasn't over yet.

Bogey Bill looked at them.

"Boo!" the goblin cried. Violet thought his voice sounded like a bullfrog's croak.

Sprite took a gold medal out of his bag. "I command you to return to the Otherworld!" he said. "I'm a Royal Pixie Tricker. Just like it says here."

Bogey Bill laughed. "You can't make me go back. I like it here. So many humans to scare!"

"Sorry we tricked your friend," Leon said, his voice shaking with fear. "I hope you're not mad at us or anything."

Bogey Bill scowled. "She wasn't my friend. So cute and smiley. Yuck!"

Violet remembered the rhyme. *If you want to trick him, make him say something sweet.* She had to try.

"But Buttercup was kind of sweet, wasn't she?" Violet asked.

Bogey Bill stuck out his tongue. "Yuck. Like a flower. Bogey Bill hates flowers."

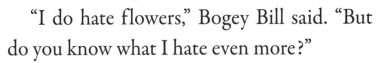

"You do?" Violet asked. Her heart sank. *This goblin doesn't think anything is sweet!* she thought.

"I do hate flowers," Bogey Bill said. "But do you know what I hate even more?"

Violet shook her head.

"Fluffy bunnies!" Bogey Bill shouted. He threw some pixie dust in the air.

Then he disappeared.

"What was he talking about?" Sprite asked.

"I don't care," Leon said. "I'm just glad he's gone."

But Violet had a bad feeling. A very bad feeling . . .

"Today is the big *Fluffy Bunny Show* live special," she said.

"So?" asked Leon.

"So, lots of kids will be watching it," Violet said. "Brittany says the show is really popular."

Sprite flew between them. "Bogey Bill will be able to scare everyone who's watching," he said. "He can send his spooky magic through the screen."

Leon's eyes got wide. "He could scare so many people!" he cried.

Violet nodded. "Right," she said. "And we will never be able to help them all! They'll be afraid of everything forever!"

Sprite fluttered up and down. "This is very, very bad," he said.

11
It's Fluffy Bunny Time!

Sprite threw pixie dust over them all. "To the TV studio!" he yelled.

In a flash, Violet, Sprite, and Leon left the creepy house.

They reappeared in the lobby of a building. The sign on the wall read "WTPX."

"We're here," Violet said. "Let's go look around."

Sprite sat on Violet's shoulder. Violet and Leon crept past the front desk.

They walked down a hallway.

Violet peeked in one door. A man stood in front of a green screen. He gave the weather report.

"That's the news studio," Violet whispered to Leon.

A woman working the lights shivered. "I hope there won't be a thunderstorm," she said. "I'm afraid of thunder and lightning."

"Bogey Bill must be here," Violet guessed. They walked to the next door.

A big pink bunny rabbit stood in front of the cameras. The bunny danced around big fake flowers made of wood.

"I'm Fluffy Bunny! Come and play with me!" sang the rabbit.

Crew members worked the lights, sound, and cameras.

Violet looked around. "Bogey Bill must be waiting to make his move."

"I don't see him," Leon said.

"Me neither. But he has got to be here somewhere," Violet said. She put Sprite into her pocket. "You'd better stay hidden. There are a lot of people in here."

Violet and Leon had found a hiding place behind a big desk. They quietly waited there.

No one noticed them. They stayed still and watched the show. Then it came time for a commercial break.

Fluffy Bunny finished his song. "Bye, bye, Bunny Buddies! I'll be back in a minute," he said.

Fluffy Bunny walked offstage. He took off his big pink bunny head.

Inside the costume was a tall, bald man.

"I'm thirsty," the man said in a deep voice. He walked out of the room. The rest of the crew followed him.

"Everyone's gone," Sprite said. "Now we can look around."

Violet started to move. Then she stopped.

"There he is!" she cried.

Hiding behind a big fake bush was a little gray goblin.

Bogey Bill!

12
Sammy Spider

"We have got to do something, fast!" Violet said.

Leon pulled the stuffed spider from his pocket. "The gnome guy gave you this, right? How are we supposed to use it?"

"He didn't tell us," Violet said. "He said we'd know what to do."

"Maybe it's a magic item," Leon said. "Like in a video game. If we touch Bogey Bill with it, he'll go back to the fairy world."

Sprite flew in front of Leon's face. "Leon, that's not how it works. Bogey Bill will only go back if we *trick* him."

"Well, I'm going to try it my way," Leon said.

Before Violet could stop him, Leon ran out onto the set. Right in front of Bogey Bill. Then he bopped the goblin on the head with the stuffed spider!

"Go back to the fairy world! Back! Back!" Leon yelled. He bopped Bogey Bill again and again.

"Leon, no!" Violet whispered.

Bogey Bill glared at Leon. "What are you doing?" he growled.

And then he smiled.

"Sammy?" Bogey Bill asked. "Sammy Spider, is that you?"

Bogey Bill grabbed the spider out of Leon's hands. He looked into its beady eyes.

Then he hugged it.

"Sammy Spider! My favorite toy!" Bogey Bill exclaimed. "I haven't seen you since I was just a little goblin."

Violet whispered to Sprite, "Robert B. Gnome told us that he

and Bogey Bill grew up together. That must be how Robert got the spider!"

Sprite nodded. "You're right!"

Bogey Bill squeezed the spider tightly. "I love you, Sammy Spider," he croaked. "You're my best friend!"

Violet grinned. "That's such a *sweet* thing to say!"

Bogey Bill looked shocked. "No fair!" he said. "I didn't mean it!"

But it was too late. The wind tunnel came for Bogey Bill. It sucked him right up.

"Happy Halloweeeeen!" Bogey Bill cried. Then he was gone.

"We did it!" Violet said happily. "We tricked him! We stopped him before he could scare everybody watching the show!"

Suddenly, Fluffy Bunny's music started up again. Fluffy Bunny ran back into the studio. The bald man put his bunny head back on.

The crew got back on set. Fluffy Bunny hopped in front of the camera.

Then Fluffy Bunny stopped hopping.
Violet gasped. "Oh no!"
Leon was hiding behind the fake flower!
He stood up.
Bright lights shone in Leon's eyes.
Fluffy Bunny stared at him.
Leon waved at the camera.
"Hi, Bunny Buddies!" Leon said.

13
More Trouble?

"**S**prite, quick!" Violet said.

Leon ran offstage. Sprite threw pixie dust on them.

"Home!" Sprite yelled.

"Achoo!" Violet sneezed. She'd forgotten to hold her nose.

In a flash, they were safe in Leon's room.

"Did you see that?" Leon asked. "I'm a star."

Leon clicked on the TV. Fluffy Bunny was talking to the camera.

"That was one of Fluffy Bunny's friends," the pink rabbit said. "Fluffy Bunny has lots of friends!"

Violet sank down to the floor.

"That was close," she said. "Sprite, let's check the book."

Sprite opened up *The Book of Tricks*. He turned to Bogey Bill's page.

Instead of a blank page, there was now a picture of the goblin.

"Thank goodness," Violet said.

Then Sprite turned to Buttercup's page. Her picture was there, too.

"We really did it!" Violet cheered.

"You mean *I* did it," Leon said. "It was *my* idea to use that spider."

"That only worked by accident!" Violet said.

"Hey, Violet and Leon!" Sprite yelled. "Stop fighting. We've got a bigger problem." He pointed to the TV screen.

It was a commercial. A man with shiny white hair and a crooked smile was talking.

"Vote for me, Wiz Finnster," said the man. "Wiz Finnster for mayor!"

"What's the big deal?" Leon asked. "That's just some old guy running for mayor."

But Violet thought she knew what was wrong.

"Wait, listen to his name," she said. "Wiz *Finn*ster. He's Finn the Wizard, isn't he?"

Sprite nodded. "That's him, all right. And if we don't stop him, he's going to be mayor of your whole town! He'll let the pixies do whatever they want, all the time!"

"Oh, great," Leon moaned.

But Violet wasn't worried.

They had already captured Pix. And Jolt. And Aquamarina.

And today, they had captured two more fairies!

They had Queen Mab to help them. And Robert B. Gnome.

Violet stood up. "I'm not afraid," she said. "We'll stop that wizard. We'll trick him and the eight other escaped pixies. And we'll do it together!"

About the Creators

Tracey West has written several book series for children, including the *New York Times*–bestselling Dragon Masters series. She is thrilled that her first series, Pixie Tricks, is being introduced to a new generation of readers.

Xavier Bonet lives in Barcelona, in a little village near the Mediterranean Sea called Sant Boi. He loves illustrating, magic, and all retro stuff. But above all, he loves spending time with his two children—they are his real inspiration.

Pixie Tricks
The Halloween Goblin

Questions and Activities

Robert B. Gnome is not afraid of Bogey Bill. Why not?

At the creepy house, Violet begins to talk loudly about how very happy she is that her hiccups are gone. Why does she do this? And does her plan work?

Before Bogey Bill disappears from the creepy house, he says that he hates fluffy bunnies. Why does this give Violet a "bad feeling"? Reread pages 69–70.

Wiz Finnster is running for mayor! Who is he, and why is Sprite worried about him? (*Psst!* If you have *The Pet Store Sprite*, look back at page 59 in that book, too!)

Bogey Bill makes everyone in Violet's class feel scared to open the closet. Have you ever felt afraid to open *your* closet? What else makes you feel scared? Draw other things that you are sometimes afraid of.